WRITTEN BY P.E. BARNES

&

ILLUSTRATED BY CAMERON WILSON

Little Owner Affirmations

I am wealthy
I am successful
I am intelligent
I am brilliant
I am resilient
I am resourceful
I am brave
I am enough
I am a born leader
I am a wonderful kid
I will be an owner

LittleOwners

<u>Dedication</u>

This book is dedicated to my husband the sports fanatic.

Thank you, for your unconditional love and support.

Stephen loved to play basketball in the local school league. He was very competitive and loved to win. He enjoyed emulating the moves of his favorite professional basketball players.

Stephen was also a great student and after finishing his school work he would attend basketball practice.

His favorite subject was math he enjoyed the challenge of algebra. Students often went to Stephen for tutoring help with their math assignments.

Stephen's Dad coached his basketball team, he really admired his Dad. He was always motivated to win because his Dad would encourage him to do his best.

He learned work ethic and commitment from his Dad.

In high school Stephen was the star player on the basketball team. He set a goal to become a professional basketball player. He knew the odds of being drafted into a professional basketball league were very slim, so he worked tirelessly to distinguish himself from the other players. He also maintained good grades in school.

Stephen was offered an athletic scholarship to a Division 1 college to play basketball. His family was so thrilled! All his hard work and dedication had finally paid off and he was able to attend his top college choice.

Stephen went to college and began playing on the basketball team as a center. His Dad was so proud of him and would attend to Stephen's games to cheer him on. He always tried to perform at his best because he knew his Dad and basketball scouts were watching him on the basketball court.

One day during a basketball game Stephen was injured badly by a member of the opposing team. The injury caused him great pain and unfortunately put an end to his basketball career. He was devastated that his dreams of becoming a professional basketball player were shattered.

Stephen was determined to complete college; he wanted to find a career that would allow him to still be in the sports field. He discussed his desires to his counselor and he suggested he consider being a sports agent. A sports agent handles the business, legal deals, and negotiates for professional athletes. Many sports agent receive between 4-10% of the athlete's contract earnings.

Stephen followed his college counselor's advice and began an internship at a local sports agency. The agency connected him with a mentor. The mentor taught him how to negotiate and introduced him to professional athletes. He dreamed of owning his own sports agency and he created a business plan. A business plan is a document that outlines how to structure, finance and grow your new business.

When Stephen graduated from college, he attended law school. After law school graduation, he took the test to become a sports agent and he passed!!! He opened his own sports agency. He helped different professional athletes in various sports fields such as basketball, baseball, and, golf. He loved helping people and became a very wealthy man. He mentored, and hired others in his community, to help them build wealth.

THE END

Vocabulary

Mentor- a more experienced or knowledgeable person advises and helps a less experienced person.

Negotiate-to deal or bargain with others in preparation for a contract or business deal.

Contract- a verbal or written formal and legally binding agreement between two or more persons.

Wealth-a great quantity of money, valuable possessions, property, or other riches.

Internship-the position of a student or trainee who works in an organization, sometimes without pay, in order to gain work experience or satisfy requirements for a qualification.

"Rich Paul Rule"

Rich Paul is the sports agent that represents LeBron James and other professional athletes. LeBron James named the rule the "Rich Paul Rule," after his agent and friend, Rich Paul. The NCAA implemented a new criteria that that requires a sports agent have a bachelor's degree amongst other requirements. The rule would have prevented Rich Paul and other agents who did not attend college from representing some of the most talented players in the world.

Made in the USA
Columbia, SC
21 September 2021